Bubby

DEBBIE WALTERS CULL

PAGE PUBLISHING, INC.
Conneaut Lake, PA

First originally published by Page Publishing 2021

ISBN 978-1-6624-4147-9 (pbk)
ISBN 978-1-6624-4146-2 (digital)

Printed in the United States of America

CHAPTER 1

"Daddy! Have you seen Shadow? I don't see her out here anywhere! Why isn't she coming when I call her?" Ten-year-old Jenny Johnson was up early that chilly Saturday morning in October. The sun was slowly melting the frost that covered the roof of their old, weathered farmhouse.

"No, honey, I haven't seen Shadow either...but I've got an idea where she might be," her father replied. Jenny's father had been up since before dawn, trying to start up the old green-and-yellow tractor parked in their gravel driveway. "See if you can find your mother and your brother, and ask them to come out here quick! I think I'll have a surprise for all of you!"

Jenny ran into the farmhouse and called, "Momma! Jake! Daddy wants you to come outside! And hurry up! He says he has a surprise for us!"

While Jenny ran back outside trying to imagine what the surprise could be, something wonderful and exciting was happening inside the Johnsons' big red barn. Shadow, their black Labrador retriever, was giving birth to a new litter of puppies. While the last puppy was being born, his two brothers and three sisters were already snuggled up next to their mother. Shadow gently nudged the puppy with her cold black nose. She licked his golden coat to clean him and welcome his arrival. As the puppies nestled up closer to get some of their mother's milk, Shadow could hear the sound of human voices coming closer.

Jenny's twelve-year-old brother, Jake, and their mother soon joined Jenny in the driveway, and all three eagerly followed Mr. Johnson into the barn. "I figured Shadow was ready to have her puppies any day, and when she wasn't in the yard this morning, I had a feeling she'd be in here," said Mr. Johnson. Shadow was anxious to show off her new puppies to her human family, and proudly thumped her tail to greet them.

"Awww, look at this real little bitty one, Daddy! It's just the cutest thing," Jenny joined in, pointing to the runt of the litter.

Mr. Johnson reached down and picked up the smallest puppy to inspect it. "It's a little boy, I see."

"Oh, Daddy, he's so sweet! Can I hold him? Will you please, please, please let me keep him?" Jenny pleaded.

Her father quickly shook his head but then hesitated and said, "We'll see, honey. We'll have to wait and see." He bent down and put the puppy back beside his mother. "Puppies are a lot of responsibility, Jenny," he added.

"I know, Daddy. But you know I'd love him and feed him and take really good care of him! I promise I will!" Jenny was doing her best to try to persuade her father as she continued. "Daddy, you said that maybe when I was ten, I could have a puppy. And my birthday was three weeks ago, so I'm ten now! And besides, I've already got a name picked out for him. I'd name him Bubby, and—"

"AND...it's time for breakfast!" her mother teased as she tugged on her daughter's long brown ponytail.

Bill and Martha Johnson were trying hard to make sure Jenny and Jake were adjusting well to their new home in the country. It had been less than a year since their Grandpa Perkins had passed away and left his farm to their parents, along with his beloved Lab, Shadow. Moving to a farm in rural Iowa was a huge change from the life they were used to over in Cedar Falls. It was a full-time job and a struggle at times for Mr. Johnson to keep his father-in-law's farm running. He had been raised in the city and had always had a good job as a certified public accountant. He'd never spent much time on a farm before, so it was a big learning experience for him. Every member of the family had to pitch in and do their part to make things work. Mrs. Johnson took in laundry and ironing jobs on occasion to bring in some extra money, and there were times when everyone had to make sacrifices in order to make ends meet. But they enjoyed working together as a family, and were proud of their accomplishments so far.

The chilly autumn days passed by quickly. The leaves changed to brilliant shades of gold, red, and yellow and fell to cover the earth like a beautiful patchwork quilt. Jake helped Jenny with the puppies by making sure they had clean straw to sleep on and plenty of fresh water to drink. And Jenny paid special attention to little Bubby as promised. Each day when she stepped off the school bus, her first stop was the barn.

"Hey there, my little Bubby! You wanna play?" Jenny giggled as Bubby stumbled through the hay and over to where she stood. She spent as much time as she could with Bubby, and they played together every day. "Bubby, I think I need to give your brothers and sisters a name too. Let me think for a minute." Jenny picked up both of the male puppies to inspect them. "I think I'll name your brothers Cooter and Scooter. Yeah, I like those names. Now what should I name your sisters?" Jenny gathered the female puppies into a little group and continued.

"Let's see... I think I'll name this one Cookie, and this one can be Cupcake. And I'll call this chocolate-colored one Brownie! There! That wasn't so hard. But now I'm hungry!" Jenny giggled and stood up to go into the house. It was almost Halloween, and she and Jake had planned to carve their pumpkins when they got home from school that day.

Bubby tugged on the cuff of her pant leg to try to keep her from leaving.

"Hey, don't worry. I'll be back later. I'll eat my supper and then I'll come see you after I'm done making my jack-o'-lantern!"

As November rolled around, the puppies started to nibble on solid food, and their teeth were coming in sharp and strong. Bubby had to settle for whatever food the other puppies left in the feeding bowl, which usually wasn't very much. So Jenny made sure he always got his share to eat, sometimes slipping him leftovers from her own dinner plate. She also made sure he got brushed every day to keep his golden coat soft and shiny and to keep the promise she made to her father.

CHAPTER 2

❧

THANKSGIVING HAD ALWAYS been a special occasion at the Johnsons'; and even though Grandpa Perkins was no longer with them, this year would be no exception. Jake and his father had a tradition of watching the Thanksgiving Day parade on television, followed by college football later in the afternoon. This year was the first time Jenny's mother let her actually help prepare the meal, instead of just cleaning up and washing the dishes afterward.

As his father flipped through the channels on the television, determined to find the best coverage of the parade, Jake was getting impatient. The aromas of roasted turkey, stuffing, homemade yeast rolls, and pumpkin pie were almost too much for Jake to bear. He hopped up off the couch and marched into the kitchen.

"How long before it's time to eat? I'm about starved to death!"

"Jake, I'll put you to work here in the kitchen if you aren't careful!" their mother joked.

Jenny chimed in, asking, "Which job do you want? Mashing the potatoes until all the lumps are gone, or stirring the gravy until your arm falls asleep?"

"Okay, okay, I'm gettin' outta here!" Jake decided he'd better go back into the other room with his father and wait to be called. Finally, it was time for the Johnsons to sit down together to enjoy their special holiday feast in their new home. Jenny put the last serving dish in its place on the big wooden farm table and then clapped her hands together as she called the family to the dining room.

"It's time to eat! Come and get it!" As they took their place around the table, everyone knew they were in for a real treat. The golden brown turkey sat steaming and waiting in front of Mr. Johnson while he finished sharpening his favorite carving knife. Before he began slicing into it, the family joined hands as he began saying the blessing. "Our heavenly Father..." As he continued, and Jenny held on to her brother and mother's hand, she bowed her head and whispered a little prayer of her own. "Dear God, thank you for my family, our home, and all this good food to eat. God bless Grandma and Grandpa Johnson, God bless Shadow and all the puppies, and please let me be able to keep little Bubby for my very own. Amen."

"Amen!"

Once the turkey was carved, the serving dishes and bowls were passed around the table. Amidst the sound of knives and forks clinking on china plates, Jake continued piling his plate full, taking some of most everything on the table.

"You forgot about the rolls, Jake," Jenny teased.

"Oh yeah. Thanks! And I almost forgot to get some cranberries!"

As always, the delicious meal that took more than five hours to prepare was gobbled down in less than half an hour.

"Man, I am so stuffed!" Jake groaned as he leaned back in his chair and stretched his arms up over his head. "I'm gonna have to come back later for a piece of that pumpkin pie!"

"Great dinner, Martha! You really outdid yourself this year," said Mr. Johnson.

"Well that's probably because Momma let me help her cook this year!" Jenny laughed.

Her father gave Jenny a wink, and smiled as he and Jake got up from the table and headed back into the family room to watch their football game. After clearing off the table and helping her mother with the dishes, Jenny gathered up a big pile of turkey scraps. She fixed Shadow her very own plate and then filled up another one for the puppies to share.

Juggling a plate in each hand, she walked out to the corner stall of the barn and sat the plates down. "Come on, you guys! Here's your Thanksgiving dinner! And Bubby, I brought some extra turkey just for you!" Shadow and her puppies gulped down every bite, wagging their tails in appreciation. Bubby licked his lips and then let out a *woof* to thank Jenny, who had started walking back to the farm house. With his belly full, Bubby plopped down next to his mother and joined his brothers and sisters for a long after-noon nap.

The cold, wintry month of December soon arrived, bringing freezing temperatures, bleak skies, and blustery northern winds along with it. Some days it just rained, and some days it snowed. The frosty snowflakes and ice crystals that clung to the barren tree branches glistened like colorful prisms in the sunshine.

During the past month, the puppies had grown bigger and stronger. They had also become very curious and were now brave enough to venture out of the barn to explore their surroundings. They especially enjoyed pouncing into the big piles of snow that drifted up against the side of the barn. Jenny liked to bundle herself up and go outside to join in on the fun. One Friday afternoon after school, she decided to give the puppies a special treat.

"Come here, you guys! I'm gonna give you all a ride on my sled!" Jenny found a blue plastic milk crate in the tool shed. She tied it onto the top of her sled with a piece of old clothesline. Then she put each puppy into the milk crate and pulled the sled out of the barn. Shadow followed behind with interest as Jenny pulled the puppies across the packed snow on the driveway and along the edge of the barnyard. Several curious cows ambled over to the fence to investigate. The puppies had never seen a cow before. Scooter and Cooter began barking loudly as they peered over the top of the milk crate and saw the strange creatures standing there.

"Jenny! What's going on over there?" her mother called out from the front porch.

"Oh, nothing. I'm taking the puppies for a sled ride. We're just trying to have some fun, that's all."

"Well, you need to come in and set the table for supper, please."

"Awww, Momma! We just got—oh, okay," she replied in dismay. "I'm sorry, you guys. Guess we'll have to do this later." She pulled the puppies back to the barn, lifted them out of the milk crate, and hung the sled up on the side of the shed. As she began to walk away, she called out, "We'll try again tomorrow! Maybe then you can have a real ride!"

CHAPTER 3

❦

JUST BEFORE BEDTIME that evening, after the Johnsons finished watching a movie together, Jenny's father made an unexpected announcement. "It's time we found homes for Shadow's pups." He walked over to the fireplace and stacked another log onto the crackling fire. "Yesterday I put an ad in the newspaper. It's the perfect time, since Christmas is only a couple of weeks away." He poked around at the logs and continued. "We shouldn't have any trouble at all selling this litter. And I'm hoping I can also sell a calf or two."

A big scowl came over Jenny's face as she put down her bowl of popcorn and listened to her father's words. *He's going to sell all of the puppies!* she thought, shaking her head in disbelief. *Did he forget? Doesn't he remember how much I want to keep Bubby?* Jenny couldn't listen to her father anymore. She let out a dismal wail as she bounded up the stairs, two at a time. Once in her bedroom, she pushed the door shut and threw herself down onto her bed. She buried her face into her pillow and soon cried herself to sleep.

As Jenny slept, her mother tiptoed into her room, took the slippers off of Jenny's feet, and then pulled her blanket up over her. She knew Jenny was sleeping but softly whispered to her daughter, "Honey, I know you're upset. But you need to understand we really need the extra money. I'm sorry, sweetheart." She quietly closed the door behind her as she left Jenny's bedroom and went downstairs.

Jenny woke up the next morning with the sun shining into her eyes through her bedroom window. *Oh good, it's Saturday!* she thought, rubbing the sleep from her eyes. She crawled out of her bed and stretched out her arms as she stood in front of her window. *I'm so glad there's no school today because that means I get to stay home and play.* But as she glanced down into the driveway, she became confused. *That looks like old Mr. Hanson out there with Jake—and he's talking to Daddy. I wonder what he wants.* Then she remembered the ad in the newspaper.

"Don't tell me people are coming here for the puppies already!" Jenny exclaimed. She quickly changed into a pair of faded blue jeans and her white knitted sweater. After pulling on some socks and boots, she bolted down the stairs.

"Jenny...wait!" her mother cried out.

"Sorry, Momma. Can't talk now!" Jenny darted through the kitchen and mudroom to the back door. She sprinted down the set of wooden steps and raced across the driveway toward the barn. She slowed down as she began to catch up with Jake, her father, and Mr. Hanson, who were now walking into the barn. Stepping into the drifted snow along the side of the barn, she tried to peek in through one of the frosted windowpanes.

Jenny tended to be very inquisitive, and wanted to know everything that was going on around her at all times. She'd gotten into trouble more than once for getting caught snooping around. Unable to see a thing, she tried her best to hear their conversation. But Jenny's curiosity compelled her to sneak around the side of the equipment shed, past the workshop, and over to the barn door. She finally managed to inch her way inside the barn so she could see and hear what they were saying.

"Well, Bill, I'll tell you what. I can take four of them off your hands. How does six hundred sound?"

Mr. Johnson thought for a minute and then replied, "Make it six twenty-five, and they're yours."

Mr. Hanson nodded and smiled, and the two men quickly shook hands to close the deal.

"Jake, would you gather up two of the males and two females, please?" For fear of being caught eavesdropping in the barn, Jenny quickly hid behind a big round bale of hay near the door and waited. Her father and Mr. Hanson left the barn and walked outside while Jake picked out four puppies as he was told.

On his way out of the barn, Jake passed right by where Jenny was hiding and said in a loud whisper, "Okay, nosy, you can come out now!" Jake carried the puppies to his father and then went off to finish his morning chores. The two men stood by Mr. Hanson's old pickup truck in the driveway, and continued their conversation. "You've got yourself some great puppies there," said Mr. Johnson. Mr. Hanson nodded in agreement as he took out his wallet. He counted out six crisp one-hundred-dollar bills, two tens, and a five and handed it to Jenny's father. Slipping the money into his coat pocket, he nodded and thanked Mr. Hanson.

"Ooh, that Jake!" Jenny muttered. How'd he know I was in here? She stepped out from behind the hay bale and raced straight over to the corner of the barn where Shadow was standing. Shadow let out a gaping yawn and stared up at her with sad brown eyes. "Awww, Shadow, I feel so sad for you. First Grandpa Perkins went away, and now most of your puppies are gone, too."

Jenny hugged Shadow around her neck and reassured her. "It'll be all right, girl. You still have two left and I'm sure hoping—" Hearing Jenny's voice, Bubby popped up out of the pile of straw. "Bubby is one of them!" she squealed. Jenny dropped down to the ground, laughing and giggling happily. Bubby, along with his little sister, jumped onto her and licked her on the face. "Awww, look! Little Brownie is still here, too! Now if we're real lucky, nobody else will want puppies for Christmas. Maybe—"

"Hey, I thought you might be out here. Where's your coat?" Jenny's father scolded. "Sorry, Daddy. I just wanted to—"

"Hurry up now and come in the house. Mom's got your breakfast ready! Besides, you could catch a cold being out here in just a sweater!" Jenny held on to her father's hand and walked with him toward the house.

As they walked, she looked up and said, "Daddy, you remembered how much I want to keep Bubby after all, didn't you?"

"Well, uhm," he replied, clearing his throat, "you know I'd like you to be able to keep him, honey. We talked about this before. We still need to wait and see, and then if nobody wants—" Their conversation ended as they walked into the kitchen for breakfast. Jenny decided to be patient and not bring up the subject again for a while. She wanted to give her father some time to think things over. *Daddy's got a lot of stuff on his mind, and I don't want to keep bugging him about it. I'll just have to wait and see what happens.*

CHAPTER 4

AFTER GOBBLING DOWN her scrambled eggs and bacon, Jenny bundled herself up properly, hurried to the barn, and called inside. "Okay, come on! It's time for that sled ride I promised!" This time she loaded up the only two puppies that were left. Shadow strutted over and joined them as they started their expedition. Bubby and Brownie stood up on their hind legs and put their front paws on the edge of the box so they could look out. "Isn't this fun, you guys?" Bubby wagged his tail as Jenny pulled the sled along the fence line and up next to the cows in the barnyard.

Jake was inside the cow pen filling up their water and feed troughs when he saw the group of them go by. Although it had taken some time, Jake was finally getting used to his new daily routine of helping his father take care of the cows and calves. He had actually come to enjoy the solitude sometimes, giving him time to collect his thoughts and ponder the future.

"Hey, I'm just about finished here. Wait up a minute so I can come with you!"

"Okay, but hurry up because the wind's picking up and I can tell it's getting colder!" Jake soon emerged from the barn carrying a snow shovel and two pair of ice skates, their shiny blades clinking together as he walked. He'd tied the laces together and had both sets of skates slung over his shoulder.

"Feel like practicing some figure eights, Jenns?"

"Oh wow! You know I do!" Jenny squealed. "Let's go!"

Shadow led the way through the field, toward the woods, and out to the pond which was now completely frozen over. As they walked, Jake had a question for his sister. "So, Jenns, I guess you're glad that man didn't take Bubby, huh?"

"I am for sure! That was a really close call!"

"Yeah, I know! You were real lucky!" he snickered. Jake had decided to keep it his own little secret that he left Bubby in the barn on purpose when he was picking out the puppies for Mr. Hanson. He knew how much Jenny loved Bubby, but he also knew next time she probably wouldn't be so lucky. As soon as they reached the pond, Jake quickly put on his skates and began shoveling the snow off the ice, a row at a time. The cold wind swirled around him, making it difficult to keep the ice cleared off.

Bubby and Brownie jumped out of the milk crate and wandered over to the pond. As Jenny finished lacing up her skates, both puppies began slipping and sliding on the ice near the pond's edge. "Come on, you guys! Follow me!" Jenny laughed as she watched them try to keep their balance on the slippery ice. Before long, Jake and Shadow joined in on the fun. Jake had found a long stick, along with a big pine cone to use as a hockey puck. Jenny and Jake passed the pine cone back and forth for a while and then Jake decided to include Shadow in their game.

"Here, Shadow! Go get it, girl!" Jake gave the pine cone a good smack with his stick and sent it skidding across the ice toward the other side of the pond. Shadow took off running, with her Bubby and Brownie chasing after her. They all ended up spinning around on the ice until Jenny skated over to help.

"Ha-ha! You guys are so funny! Hey, Jake, did you see them?"

"Yeah, I saw. And I see it's starting to drizzle!" Jenny let out a big groan to show her disappointment.

"Dang it, Jake! Can you believe it? I guess we're gonna have to go home already."

"Yeah, I guess so," Jake agreed. "Glad I went to all that trouble to shovel off the pond," he added, with a hint of sarcasm. "But it's just as well, I guess, 'cause I just remembered I've only got two days to finish a book report that's due on Monday! Yikes!"

"Yeah, I've still got some more homework to do, too," said Jenny. "And then it's only one more week till Christmas vacation! Yippee!" After Jenny took off her skates and put her boots back on, she lifted Bubby and Brownie back into the crate for the ride home on the sled. This time, Jenny carried the skates and shovel, and Jake pulled the sled as they hurried across the field. The drizzle turned into freezing rain, and the wind steadily picked up. After finally making it back to their yard, the puppies jumped out of the crate and followed Shadow into the barn. Jake hung up the sled, and Jenny put up their skates.

"Don't worry, we'll have plenty more chances to go back to the pond. See you guys later," Jenny called out, as she and Jake left the barn and raced each other to the house.

CHAPTER 5

❦

IT WASN'T UNTIL the following Sunday that anyone else called or came to see about the puppies. Upon returning home from church, the Johnsons saw an unfamiliar car parked in their driveway. A nicely dressed man and his plump matronly wife opened their car doors and stepped out. The man smiled pleasantly as he walked toward the Johnsons' truck, with his frowning wife staying close by his side.

He looks friendly enough, Jenny thought. *But I'm not so sure about that lady. She looks pretty grumpy! And she's wrinkling up her nose like she smells something bad!* Having been on the farm for a while now, Jenny was used to the pungent odor of cow manure and thought nothing of it. Jenny couldn't help noticing the collar on the woman's fur coat, complete with about half a dozen little animal heads. She was certain their glazed-over eyes were staring right at her. *What in the world? What are those things? Ferrets? Eww, maybe they're weasels! Where would a person ever get a coat that looks like that?*

Her concentration on the mysterious heads was abruptly broken when a rear car door opened, and out came a young, blond-haired boy. He looked to be around Jenny's age, and was dressed in a dark-blue military school uniform and matching coat.

"Walter! I told you to stay in the car!" the woman scolded. "You might step into some mud, or something worse, and those shoes are brand-new!" Jenny's father was amused, and tried to keep a straight face as he welcomed the visitors.

"Well, hello there! I'm Bill Johnson. What can I do for you folks?"

"Albert Williams here. Pleasure to meet you." He exchanged a friendly handshake with Jenny's father. "We were driving by on our way back to the city when we noticed your sign up on the road about the puppies for sale. Our son insisted we stop." The man glanced down at the ground and continued. "If it's not too much trouble, do you suppose we could take a look?"

"Well, yes, you sure can. We only have two left, though. They're in the barn right over there. Follow me." Jenny's father turned and began walking toward the barn.

"Well, ahem, excuse me!" the woman objected. "You don't really expect us to walk into that nasty, smelly barn do you? You're just going to have to bring them out here instead!"

"Oh, of course! I'm sorry, ma'am. Jenny, please go get the puppies and bring them out here for these folks."

Jenny could not believe what her father was asking her to do. She felt such a sense of sadness come over her. It was hard for her to even comprehend what was happening. Grudgingly, she obeyed her father, but she was in no hurry as she walked in a zigzag pattern toward the barn. She kicked a big chunk of gravel as she went. As she walked up to Bubby and Brownie, big tears welled up in her eyes. The puppies were having fun playing tug-of-war with a piece of bailing twine they had found. *Maybe I could tell Daddy I couldn't find Bubby.* But that would not be the truth, and Jenny knew it was wrong to tell a lie. So she gathered up both puppies, one under each arm; and with much reluctance, she walked back to where the group was waiting.

The young boy watched Jenny closely as she approached. She was clutching both puppies tightly, looking down at the ground and trying not to make eye contact with anyone. *Oh, if they're going to take a puppy, please let them take the girl puppy! Please let them take little Brownie and not Bubby!*

Mr. Johnson started explaining to the man, "Now the little golden male there is the runt of the litter, but the chocolate female is a very healthy pup, and I think—"

"I want both of them, Mummy!" the boy interrupted.

"Walter! Why would you ever want two puppies?" his father objected. "You know once you go back to the academy, your mother and I will be left to take care of them, and—"

"Shhh, Albert! Be quiet and let Walter have both of them if that's what he wants!"

"But dear..." Realizing it would be useless to argue with his wife, the henpecked husband accepted defeat and said, "I guess we'll take them both, if you agree. How much do we owe you?"

"Well, let me see here..." Mr. Johnson thought for a minute before replying. "I'll let you have them for two hundred and twenty-five dollars each."

Suddenly Jake started to interrupt, "But, Dad! That's a lot more than—" Mr. Johnson coughed into his fist and put his other arm around Jake as if to hug his son. As his father began to squeeze his shoulder, Jake finally got the hint to keep quiet.

"Two hundred twen—why that would be four hundred and fifty dollars! I—I had no idea puppies cost that much these days!" the man exclaimed, as he gave his wife a disgruntled look.

"Albert, will you just pay the man! It's such a small price to pay to make little Walter happy! Just think of them as more Christmas presents!" Mr. Williams knew there was no use in trying to reason with his wife. He shook his head in defeat and scribbled out a check for the full amount. Jenny had been watching in horror and sadly protested.

"Daddy! No! I can't believe you're doing this!" Her father shot her a disapproving glance.

Through her tears, she patted Brownie on her head and unwillingly gave her to the boy. "Goodbye, little Brownie. You be a good girl. I'm sure gonna miss you!"

Then she sadly gave her little Bubby one last hug and kiss. Bubby responded with a big wet lick on Jenny's cheek. His tail wagged as he looked up at her with his big brown eyes. Still in disbelief, Jenny sobbed loudly as she handed Bubby to her father, instead of the boy. She was so upset she couldn't even speak to say goodbye to Bubby. Then she turned around, ran frantically toward the farmhouse, and bolted up the backstairs.

In the solitude of her bedroom, she stood alone at the window and cried uncontrollably. Her tears blurred her vision and burned into her cheeks as she waved at the car in despair.

"Goodbye, Bubby Johnson. I love you! I love you, and I'm so sorry you have to go." Jenny watched helplessly as the fancy car began driving away. Both puppies were struggling to see out the rear window as the car pulled out of the driveway. Poor little Bubby could barely see his mother, Shadow, who was now sadly walking back to the barn with her head held low.

CHAPTER 6

———— ❦ ————

JENNY REFUSED TO come down for Sunday dinner when her mother called her. Instead, she spent the entire afternoon in her bedroom. When she wasn't crying, she was sleeping. When she wasn't sleeping, she stared blankly out of her bedroom window and rocked back and forth in her rocking chair. She wouldn't come down for supper that night either.

"I'm not hungry," she told her mother when she called her to come eat.

"Bill, I'm really getting worried about Jenny," her mother said as they sat down at the kitchen table. "She barely touched her breakfast before church this morning. She hasn't really eaten anything since supper last night."

"Martha, I think you're overreacting." Mr. Johnson passed the bowl of mashed potatoes to Jake and continued. "She'll snap out of it. It may just take a little time." Mr. Johnson made some room on his plate and helped himself to a piece of fried chicken. "Anyway, I thought maybe Jake and I could drive out to the back woods and round up a Christmas tree when we're finished with supper. You know how Jenny loves to decorate the tree every year." He spooned out a second helping of green beans. "Wouldn't she like that?"

"I sure hope you're right; but I'm pretty sure it's going to take a lot more than a Christmas tree to get Jenny through this."

"All right, then! Let's get going!"

Mr. Johnson fired up the old flatbed pickup truck, while Jake grabbed a chainsaw out of the shed. Shadow invited herself along for the trip and jumped up onto the bed of the truck. It was a cold and bumpy ride across the icy ruts in the empty cornfield. Their journey continued on, past the frozen pond, through a large hay field, and over to a big grove of cedar trees. Leaving the truck running and the headlights on, they began their pursuit for the "perfect" tree. As they searched, Jake asked his father a question that had been on his mind since that morning.

"So, Dad. How come you sold Bubby and Brownie for so much more money than you did all the other puppies? Wasn't that being dishonest?"

Mr. Johnson grinned and replied, "Well, no, son, it was definitely not being dishonest. It's because Mr. Hanson bought four puppies and so I gave him a quantity discount. Sort of like a package deal. Besides, Mr. Williams still got a fair deal."

While Jake pondered his father's explanation, Shadow began barking. She stood next to a beautiful cedar tree that was exactly what they had been looking for. It was big, bushy, and stood about eight feet tall. "Oh, yeah! That's an awesome tree, Shadow!" Jake applauded. Mr. Johnson agreed, cranked up the chainsaw, and began cutting down the tree. The smell of the freshly cut cedar filled the air. Once the buzzing of the chainsaw stopped, there was a sudden snap of the tree trunk, a big whoosh, and then a hearty thump as it collapsed to the ground.

"Okay, Jake! Give me a hand here and we'll get this beauty loaded up." Jake helped his father lift the tree onto the truck.

"This is pretty cool, getting to cut down our own tree for a change," Jake said.

"Yes, I guess that's one benefit of living on your own farm, huh?" his father added.

"Yep! And I can think of another one too."

"Oh? What would that be, Jake?"

"Having lots of wide open spaces!" Jake paused briefly, took a deep breath, and then continued, "So, Dad, I don't suppose you'd let me drive the truck back to the house, would you? I don't see much traffic out here. Ha-ha!" Jake began tying the tree down to the bed of the truck with a long piece of rope.

"Well...I suppose. I don't have a problem with that."

"Cool! Thanks, Dad!" Jake finished tying off the tree and then ran up and jumped into the driver's seat. Although he had to stretch his neck to see over the top of the steering wheel, he smiled from ear to ear.

"You know, Jake, it's hard to believe in just a few more years you'll be old enough for your learner's permit!" Mr. Johnson shut his door, reminded Jake to fasten his seat belt as he buckled himself in, and added, "You're growing up so fast, son!"

"Yeah, I keep trying to tell everybody I'm not a little kid anymore!"

Mr. Johnson stuck his head out of the window and let out a loud, two-fingered whistle for Shadow. She quickly came running, jumped up onto the truck's flatbed with enthusiasm, and sat next to "her" tree.

"Whenever you're ready, Jake," said Mr. Johnson. "Just take it slow and get a feel for it. It's an automatic instead of a stick shift, so you don't have to worry about working a clutch or shifting gears."

Jake put the truck into D for drive and cleared his throat. He could barely reach the gas and brake pedals, but he gripped the steering wheel firmly with both hands and began driving back to the house. Things went pretty smoothly through the hay field, but every time Jake drove over a frozen rut in the cornfield, the truck bounced up and then came back down with a thud. Each time, it sent Shadow flying up into the air. She finally jumped down from the bed of the truck and took off running toward the barn. Mr. Johnson chuckled and thought, *I need to ask Santa for a new pair of shock absorbers for Christmas!*

And Jake was thinking, *Man, this is fun! This is so easy! I don't know why everybody thinks knowing how to drive is such a big deal. I'm doing it now, and I bet I can already drive good enough to pass a driver's test. I want to just hurry and be a grown-up!*

CHAPTER 7

THE SOUND OF Christmas music and the aroma of the cinnamon from freshly baked Snickerdoodle cookies crept upstairs and coaxed Jenny out of her bedroom. Having cried until there were no tears left, there was an emptiness inside her like she'd never felt before. Jenny splashed some cool water onto her face from the bathroom sink. Her puffy red eyes stared back as she peered into the mirror. She ran a brush through her hair, and put it up into pigtails.

Jenny tiptoed down the stairs and over to where her father and brother were setting the cedar tree into its stand. She quietly looked around the room and then whispered, "Pretty tree."

"Well, there's my girl!" her father welcomed her.

"Oh, sweetie. You must be starving! I saved you a plate from supper," her mother said. Jenny didn't appear to be interested as she looked away and shook her head. "Okay, well then how about a nice cup of cocoa and some of your favorite cookies? I just took a batch out of the oven. They're still warm."

Jenny couldn't resist her mother's homemade cookies, and she realized she hadn't eaten since the night before. So in between sipping on her cocoa and nibbling on Snickerdoodles, she watched her brother hang strings of colored lights on the tree. Half-heartedly, Jenny decided to help decorate the tree. She opened a box full of beautiful, shiny ornaments. Many of them had been in the Johnson family since before Jake was born.

"You know, Christmas is less than a week away, Jenny," her mother pointed out. As hard as she tried to seem uninterested in the Christmas festivities, Jenny couldn't help responding to her mother with a small bit of excitement.

"I've been saving up my allowance all year long so I can buy something really nice for everybody." She thought for a moment and then added, "Since we're on Christmas break, maybe you could drive us to town so we could do our shopping tomorrow!"

"That is exactly what I had in mind! And it would be so much fun!" her mother replied. She hoped her daughter was beginning to cheer up a little.

Jenny carefully removed the tissue paper from a green and red ornament with "Baby Jenny's First Christmas" imprinted in gold letters. She hung it on the front of the tree, on a branch down near the bottom. Jenny tried to keep her mind on helping with the decorations, but as hard as she tried, she just couldn't stop thinking about little Bubby. She kept picturing his sad little face trying to look out the back window of that car. *He'll be spending his first Christmas with strangers. There's no way that boy could ever love Bubby the way I do. He never could, and he never will.*

The next day turned out to be a better one for Jenny. It was filled with excitement and anticipation, which helped lift Jenny's spirits. While Mr. Johnson took some calves to the livestock auction over at the stockyards, the rest of the family went into downtown Cedar Falls. This is where her family had traditionally done their Christmas shopping in the past. It always managed to put Jenny in the mood for shopping. For some reason, she liked shopping on the old town square a lot more than at the mall on the edge of town.

A damp chill hovered in the air, and the flurries of snow and songs of the carolers on the sidewalks provided the perfect atmosphere for getting into the Christmas spirit.

"Okay, check your watches," said Mrs. Johnson. "It's ten o'clock. I'll meet you guys here in front of Murphy's at twelve noon."

"That gives us two hours, Jake," Jenny said.

"Wow, Jenns! Thanks for telling me because I didn't know that," Jake replied sarcastically.

"Come on, you two. Behave yourselves, and be back here on time!" their mother instructed.

"Don't worry, we will," they agreed.

Jenny and Jake quickly hurried off in separate directions. With a basket full of freshly baked loaves of banana bread, Mrs. Johnson left to visit the Cedar Village Retirement Home that was nearby. Every year, she baked something special for the elderly residents; and for many of them, it was the highlight of their holiday season.

Luckily, Jenny managed to put her unhappiness aside as she roamed from store to store. She passed by three different Santa Clauses ringing their bells. It reminded her of how Grandpa Perkins used to explain why there were so many Santa Clauses around at Christmas. He would tell her, "Well, you see, it's because they've all been deputized! They're all deputy Clauses helping out the real Santa Claus, because he has to be up at the North Pole supervising the elves while they make the toys!" It all made perfect sense to Jenny.

"Merry Christmas!" she called out as she dropped some coins into each of their buckets; and each time, she closed her eyes and made a special wish. At Corner's Book Store, she found a set of books about mythical dragons for Jake. And at Cole's Department Store next door, she bought a pretty blue bathrobe and a matching pair of fuzzy slippers she hoped her mother would like.

But Jenny was having a hard time deciding what to get her father. *Jake will get Daddy another tie again this year, I just know it!* Jenny chuckled, remembering how her father had a surprised look on his face every year when he opened those ties. *Oh wait, I know what I can do! Daddy was talking to Mr. Harper after church last week about a fishing pole he liked at his store. I'll see if Mr. Harper remembers what kind it was.*

She walked two blocks down to an old brick building on the corner and peered through the store's front window. There she noticed a small handwritten sign that said Big Sale Tomorrow. Jenny grinned as she realized she couldn't remember a time when that sign wasn't on the window. As she opened the big wooden door at Harper's Sporting Goods, a little bell jingled to announce her arrival. Struggling to close the heavy door behind her, she noticed a slight musty smell inside the dimly lit store. The timber floors creaked as she walked over to a glass display counter, where an elderly gentleman was standing. He greeted her with a nod and a friendly smile.

"Hello, Mr. Harper! Boy I sure hope you can help me."

"I'll do my best, Miss Jenny. What can I do for you?"

"Well, I'm pretty sure I heard you and my daddy talking after church last Sunday. He was saying something about a fishing pole he really liked. Do you remember which one it was?"

"Hmm, listening in, were you?" Jenny blushed as Mr. Harper continued. "Why yes, I believe I do remember the one! Come over here with me." She followed Mr. Harper to a large rack where he pointed out a shiny black rod and reel with red trim and silver lettering. "This is the one. It's an Ugly Stik!"

Jenny giggled. "I don't think it's ugly! I think it's pretty!"

"No, no! That's the name of it. An Ugly Stik. Whatever it's called, I'm sure your father would like fishing with it."

Jenny giggled. "Oh, I think so too, Mr. Harper. Yes, I do want to buy it for Daddy. Ooh, he's going to be so surprised!" Mr. Harper rang up her purchase on his big antique cash register and slid the money into the cash drawer. After fumbling around in the back room for a couple of minutes, he reappeared with the box the fishing rod came in. He put the rod into its box and closed it up tightly.

"Sorry, but I don't have a bag this will fit into!" He laughed. He handed the long box to Jenny as she picked up her other packages. She started walking toward the door to leave, but then she happened to glance over toward a shelf full of pet supplies. *Oh no, I almost forgot! I still want to get Shadow something for Christmas. She's part of our family, too!* While looking over the large assortment of items on the shelf, Jenny's eyes fell upon a beautiful emerald-green collar made of leather. *I bet this would be just the right size.*

She sat all of her packages back down onto the floor and glanced quickly at the price tag on the collar. Then Jenny opened up her purse and took out her wallet to see how much money she had left. She let out a big sigh as she pulled out the last of her spending money. Mr. Harper couldn't help but overhear her sigh. He noticed her clutching a five-dollar bill, and walked over to where she stood.

"You seem disappointed. Is something wrong?"

"Well, I wanted to buy this collar for our dog, Shadow, but the price tag says it costs ten dollars!"

"What? Ten dollars? Let me see that tag!" Mr. Harper reached into his shirt pocket and took out his black marker. Then he wrote through the price on the tag, changing the ten to a five. "Looks like I forgot to mark this one down. This collar is supposed to be on sale for half price!"

"Oh! Half price? Then I have enough money after all!" exclaimed Jenny. Jenny jabbered excitedly as she paid for Shadow's present. She slipped her wallet and Shadow's collar into her purse, checked to see what time it was, and then picked up her packages again.

"It's ten minutes till twelve! I've really got to go! Thanks again, Mr. Harper, and Merry Christmas!"

"And the same to you, Miss Jenny!" he replied, with a contented smile on his face and a twinkle in his eye.

CHAPTER 8

"HEY, JAKE," MRS. Johnson called. "Will you please hang up these Christmas cards for me? It looks like we've got about ten new ones here!"

"Sure, Mom! Hand 'em here." Jake took the roll of tape and stack of cards from his mother. He began taping them up over the arched doorway leading from the front hallway into the family room. This was another holiday tradition the Johnsons wanted to hold on to now that they were living on the farm. It was always fun to check the mail each day to see who they'd received cards from.

With Christmas quickly approaching, there were plenty of things to do to keep the family busy. Mrs. Johnson took care of the house, as usual, but also did the special holiday cooking and baking. In addition to her regular cleaning, she also took in some extra laundry jobs from some folks in town. When Mr. Johnson wasn't tending to the cattle or delivering hay, he was cutting down trees and splitting up logs for firewood. He had picked up some bookkeeping jobs that took up his time as well.

Jake kept the snow shoveled off the porches, steps, and walkways around the farmhouse, in addition to his other chores out in the barnyard. Most of Jenny's time was spent helping her mother however she could. And she spent hours repositioning the gifts she'd bought so they were exactly where she wanted them under the tree.

When Christmas Eve finally arrived, Jenny was making one last inspection of all the packages, examining and shaking the ones with her name on them. As she crawled on her hands and knees around to the rear of the tree, the doorbell rang.

"Can you get the door, honey?" Jenny's mother called from the kitchen. "My fingers are covered with cookie dough!"

"Sure. In just a second, Momma." Jenny crawled from the Christmas tree over to the front door. Still on her hands and knees, she reached up and awkwardly turned the knob, and opened the door to a big surprise. "Grandma and Grandpa! Momma! Grandma and Grandpa Johnson are here!" Jenny jumped to her feet so she could give each of her grandparents a big hug around the neck.

"We were going to wait until morning to surprise you, but we decided to spend the night here instead," her grandma explained.

"I'm just kind of confused, because nobody told me you were coming for Christmas!" Jenny's mother came into the front hallway from the kitchen, drying her hands on a terry cloth towel. After welcoming her in-laws, she began explaining it all to Jenny.

"Well, honey, it was sort of a spur-of-the-moment thing. We wanted to do something to help cheer you up. We thought a visit from Grandma and Grandpa might help." Grandpa poked his head into the kitchen.

"Mmmmmm! I'm most certain I detect the aroma of chocolate chip cookies baking in the oven!" Then he shuffled from the hallway over to the fireplace to warm his weathered hands. About that same time, Jake and his father came in from the workshop and joined everyone in the family room.

"Well, hello, Mother! Hi, Pop! I was hoping you guys would show up tonight!" Jenny's father put his hand on his dad's shoulder while giving him a hearty handshake. Then he grabbed his mother's hands and gave her a big kiss on her cheek.

Jake chimed in, "Wow, Gramps! Am I glad to see you!"

"Well, well, well! Butter me up and call me a biscuit!" Jake laughed as his grandpa continued. "Jacob William, you are growin' so fast! You're gonna be as tall as me before very long." Then he turned to Jenny and gently pinched her cheeks. "And as for you, Miss Jennifer Rose, you are quite the beauty! You're almost as pretty as your grandma!"

"Oh, Grandpa!" The kids groaned and blushed. They didn't mind their grandpa calling them by both names. "The only time Momma and Daddy use our middle name is if we're in trouble for something," Jenny explained.

Grandpa laughed and then said, "Well, I'll be sure to make a note of that for future reference!" After catching up on the latest family news and enjoying some fresh coffee and cookies in the kitchen, Grandpa stood up from his chair and strolled back into the family room.

"Well, listen here, kiddos! On our way over from the airport, me and your Grandma—err, Grandma and I—drove by a church where they were setting things up for a nativity scene tonight."

"And we thought you kids might want to go see it with us," Grandma added. "We'll take that sporty race car they gave us at the rental place."

"So, who's up for the adventure?" Grandpa asked. Jake and Jenny both scrambled to put on their coats and hats and rushed out the front door. "We'll take that as a yes!" Grandpa laughed. "See you after a while, Bill! You sure you don't want to come along?"

"That's okay, Pop! You and Mother go on and have fun!"

A crowd of people had already gathered at the First Baptist Church to hear the story of the birth of Jesus. The Johnsons walked over near the main entrance of the church where the manger scene was set up, and where others already stood. A life-size baby doll lay in a straw-filled crib, next to some church members dressed in costumes. Two of them played the parts of Mary and Joseph, and others were dressed as shepherds, angels, and wise men. A real live donkey and a couple of goats were grazing on the grass next to the manger. As more people arrived, they too walked up to the manger scene and stood quietly.

The crowd waited for the church pastor to begin reciting Luke 2:10–11 from the Bible. Jenny gazed up at the stars in the night sky and listened as the pastor began. "And the angel said unto them, 'Fear not: for, behold, I bring you good tidings of great joy, which shall be to all people. For unto you is born this day in the city of David a Saviour, which is Christ the Lord.'"

Jenny reached up to grab her grandpa's rugged hand, and smiled as her grandma took her other hand. As she listened to the story, she became filled with a sense of inner peace and happiness. A warm glow came over her, as the words from the Bible helped remind her of the true meaning of Christmas. At the end of the program, the crowd sang some Christmas carols and wished each other a Merry Christmas. Soon everyone could be seen hurrying to their cars and trucks, disappearing into the darkness of the night.

On the way home, Grandpa took his time driving around in some nearby neighborhoods so they could all see the pretty Christmas lights and decorations. Before long, he pulled up to the Johnsons' farmhouse. The temperature had dropped sharply since they'd left, so they all hurried to get inside where it was warm.

"Yoo-hoo! We're home!" Grandma shouted out.

"And Grandpa let us get peppermint ice cream cones at the Dairy Barn on the way home!" Jake announced.

"Can you believe that, as cold as it is?" Jenny asked. "And we even got to stand up on the back seat and stick our bodies out the moon roof so we wouldn't get ice cream all over the inside of the car!"

As Jenny's mom raised her eyebrows in shock, she cleared her throat and replied, "Well, umm, I suppose grandparents are allowed to let their grandchildren do things like that." Trying to remain calm, she continued. "It sounds like you had a really nice time! But maybe next time you should just get milkshakes!" She winked at her father-in-law and smiled.

"Well, it's getting pretty late, so you guys had better hurry up and get to bed now so Santa Claus can come," their father added. Without any argument, the children said their good nights, and made sure their stockings were still in place. They hurried upstairs into their bedrooms, wondering if they'd be able to fall asleep.

As Jenny lay restlessly in her bed, she could hear the cheerful voices of her parents and grandparents downstairs. The kitchen was right below Jenny's bedroom, so it was hard to ignore them. *Aren't they ever going to go to bed? We have to get up early in the morning to open our presents!* Jenny had just begun to nod off to sleep when she very clearly heard the word puppies. As usual, her curiosity kicked in, so she jumped out of her bed and crouched down onto the floor. She put her ear next to the heat register so she could listen in. But it was hard for her to make out everything they were saying.

"Bill! Shh! She'll hear you! Her bedroom's right above us, and you know how she likes to eavesdrop," her mother cautioned. The voices then became muffled, so Jenny couldn't hear their conversation any more.

"I suppose Daddy's telling them about how he sold Bubby and the other puppies," she mumbled softly. Jenny crawled back into her bed and pulled her warm blanket and quilt up over her. She peeked out over the covers toward her window, and noticed flurries of snow had begun floating down from the sky. They say Christmas snow is magic snow. Jenny closed her eyes and sadly began drifting off to sleep. *Merry Christmas, little Bubby—wherever you are.*

CHAPTER 9

❦

IT WAS STILL dark when Jake knocked on his sister's bedroom door. When she didn't answer, he quietly knocked again, opened the door, and then walked into her room and over to her bed.

"Psst! Wake up!" Jake whispered as he shook Jenny's shoulder. Jenny turned over in her bed, rubbed her eyes, and yawned. She squinted her eyes and looked up at Jake. Then, remembering what day it was, she quickly scrambled out of her bed.

"Oh my gosh! Christmas morning's finally here!" Throwing on her robe and slippers, Jenny followed Jake as he crept quietly down the stairs, trying not to wake everyone else in the house. To their surprise, both their father and grandpa were already up and dressed and waiting downstairs. Grandpa poked at the glowing embers in the fireplace while their father topped them with some more firewood. Mrs. Johnson and Grandma soon joined them all in the family room.

"We thought you two were going to sleep all day!" Grandpa teased. "And hey, guess what! Looks like you've got yourselves a white Christmas this year." Jenny and Jake's eyes lit up as they peered out the window at the blanket of fresh snow glistening in the fading moonlight.

"And you might want to check out your Christmas stockings over there," said Grandma. The children took their stockings down from the mantle and looked inside. Each stocking was filled with candy bars, a couple of oranges, and apples. Jake also pulled out a new Duncan yo-yo and a pocket knife Grandpa had slipped into his stocking. A beautiful golden locket was in Jenny's stocking, along with three different colors of nail polish and a Magic 8-Ball.

"A Magic 8-Ball! Wow! I love Magic 8-Balls! They're so much fun." Jenny closed her eyes, silently asked her secret question, and turned the 8-Ball over to see the answer. "Reply hazy, try again. I wonder what that means!"

Then their father called out, "Okay, guys, come on over here and see what else Santa Claus brought you!"

Jake plopped down beside Jenny in front of the tree and said, "Dad! Now you know we don't really believe in Santa Claus anymore, right? That's just kid stuff!"

"Oh, I see. Well then, I guess you're not interested to see what's in here," his father teased, as he shook one of Jake's presents from side to side. Jake grinned and grabbed the package from his father. He quickly unwrapped the long oblong-shaped box to find another cardboard box stapled shut at both ends. Using his new pocket knife, he carefully pried up the staples and opened one end of the box. He pulled out a brand-new rifle and carrying case.

"Oh, man! I can't believe it! A single-shot .22 caliber! It's the exact one I've been wanting!"

His father laughed and said, "Well, I guess Santa Claus did pretty good after all! Tomorrow, Grandpa and I can go out in the field with you."

"I can't wait!" cried Jake, hugging his father and then his grandpa.

"We'll brush up on safety rules later today, and then tomorrow you can practice shooting," his father said.

"Okay, now let's have Jenny open one of her presents," her mother suggested.

"How about this one?" Jenny asked. She opened up a small blue velvet box she'd had her eye on and peeked inside. "Look! It's my birthstone ring!" She slipped it onto her finger and admired the sparkling blue sapphire stone. "It fits perfectly. Oh, I just love it!"

As both children continued opening their presents, brightly colored wrapping paper, ribbons, and bows flew in every direction. Jake got a pair of leather boots, some blue jeans, a gray flannel hoodie, and some ammunition for his new rifle. Thanking Jenny for the dragon books, he handed her the present he'd bought her. It was a beginner artist's set, with colored pencils, watercolors, and some oil paints.

"Jake! This must have cost you an arm and a leg!" Jenny said.

Jake pulled his right arm up inside his sweater and joked, "Murphy's had it on sale, so it only cost me an arm!" Jenny laughed and wrinkled up her nose at her brother. Then she opened her other presents to find some sweaters and leggings, a pair of fringed cowboy boots, and a Scrabble board game.

Grandma handed Jake and Jenny a present each and said, "Here's a little something from your grandpa and me." They unwrapped the packages, and a silence fell over the room as they stared down at the presents from their grandparents. Grandma couldn't understand the puzzled looks on their faces, so she asked them to hold the presents up so she could see them. Everyone burst out laughing when they realized Grandma had gotten their presents mixed up with the other's.

"Here, Jake. You'll probably be needing this razor and shaving cream before I will!" Jenny laughed.

"I sure hope so! And here, you can have my strawberry hand lotion!" Once he was able to stop laughing, Jake said, "Okay, Mom and Dad! Open the ones from me next, please! I sure hope I didn't get 'em mixed up like Grandma did!"

Jake's mom grinned as she went first. He had picked out a fancy bottle of perfume and a wicker basket filled with colored soaps and bath oil beads from Stanley's drugstore. She dabbed a little of the perfume behind both ears. "Mmmmm, this smells so nice...like orange blossoms and honey! Thank you, sweetie!"

Then Jake's father took his turn, first opening a bottle of his favorite cologne. In the second box was a brown necktie with a blue and green duck on it.

"A new tie... What a nice surprise, son!"

Jenny giggled when she saw it and said, "You needed a new tie, huh, Daddy!" He winked and grinned as he thanked Jake and put it on over his bathrobe.

It was Jenny's turn now to give her parents their gifts. Jenny's mother opened hers and hurried to try it on. "Ooh, look at me!" She laughed as she pretended to be a model, strutting around the room wearing her new bathrobe and slippers.

"You look beautiful, Momma. Here you go, Daddy. This one is yours!" Mr. Johnson looked at the long, narrow package.

"I wonder if it's another new tie," he kidded. As he tore back the paper carefully, his face lit up when he opened up the box and took one look at his new fishing rod. "Jenny, you must have been reading my mind! How did you know?"

"Well, I had some help, Daddy, thanks to Mr. Harper."

"I don't know what to say other than thank you, and I can't wait to try out my new Ugly Stik!"

Jokingly, Grandpa said, "Before you do, I should go out to the pond and warn the fish. Ugly but deadly. It's only fair."

"Oh thanks, Pop! Appreciate that!" While the adults finished exchanging gifts, Jake and Jenny thanked everyone again for their presents, and claimed they'd gotten exactly what they wanted. But Jenny knew in her heart the only thing she really wanted wasn't under the Christmas tree.

"Hey, Jenny, don't you still have one more gift to deliver?" her mother asked.

"Oh yeah, you're right! I almost forgot about Shadow's present!" Jenny hurried to get dressed and then quickly put on her winter jacket, boots, and hat. She reached under the tree and grabbed the last wrapped package, secretly slipping her Magic 8-Ball into her coat pocket. With Shadow's gift in hand, she rushed out the back door. "I'll be in the barn!" she called over her shoulder.

CHAPTER 10

———— ❦ ————

THE NEW SNOW crunched under her rubber boots as she walked. She tried her best to avoid the snowdrifts in her path. As soon as Shadow saw Jenny come into the barn, she began wagging her tail. "Hey there, girl! You didn't think I'd forget you on Christmas morning, did you? I've got something very special for you." Jenny sat down next to Shadow and carefully unwrapped the package. "Here, let's try it on you."

She put the collar around Shadow's smooth, shiny neck. It fit her perfectly, just as Jenny imagined it would. Tears slowly began to well up in her eyes as she wrapped her arms around Shadow. Unable to hold back her tears any longer, she began to cry. She stroked Shadow's soft black coat and ran her fingers across the beautiful emerald-green collar which seemed to have been made especially for Shadow. "I'm trying real hard not to be sad today. I know everybody wants me to be happy because it's Christmas. They've all tried to cheer me up and help take my mind off of Bubby, but I just can't."

Jenny wished she could stay out in the barn with Shadow because she didn't really want to go back into the house where she had to smile and pretend to be happy. She took her Magic 8-Ball out of her pocket and showed it to Shadow. "Look what I got! I asked it a question earlier, but

I think it said to ask again later. So here goes!" Jenny closed her eyes and asked her question once more. Turning the 8-Ball over, she read the message "You may rely on it."

It was at that moment Jenny swore she could hear a faint "yip, yip, yip" off in the distance. *Oh, I'm just imagining things.* She heard it again, but this time it was closer and louder. All at once, Jenny was pounced on by a ball of soft golden fur. "Ohhhh! Oh my gosh! I can't believe this! It's Bubby! It really is Bubby, and he really has come home, just like I wished for!" Jenny's sad tears quickly became happy tears.

Bubby was licking her in the face, and wagging his tail a mile a minute. Jenny then heard some more noises behind her. She turned around toward the door of the barn. There stood her parents, her grandparents, and Jake, all with big happy smiles on their faces. "MERRY CHRISTMAS, Jenny!" they shouted.

"Oh, Momma, Daddy," Jenny cried. "I can't believe it! That Magic 8-Ball really works!" Jenny's father laughed as he offered her his hand.

"Come on, honey. We'll all go back into the house and I'll try to explain everything." Holding Bubby close to her, Jenny grabbed her father's hand and stood up. Mr. Johnson turned back toward Shadow and called to her. "Come on, girl! You can come too!"

By now, the sun was rising and revealing the beautiful blanket of fresh snow that covered the ground. Once the family made it back inside the warm house, Jenny's father began to explain what had happened the night before. "So remember when you all went out last night to see the nativity scene?" Jenny smiled and nodded her head. "Well, while you were gone, Mr. Williams came here to see if I would consider taking Bubby back." Mr. Johnson cleared his throat as he continued. "He told me his son, I think his name is Walter, lost interest in the puppies once they got home. Bubby wouldn't eat because he was sad, and Mr. Williams said he hated to see Bubby so miserable. He knew his boy didn't deserve to have a pet in the first place, and evidently his son admitted he really didn't want Bubby."

"Then why did he say he wanted him if he really didn't want him?" Jenny asked.

"Because he could see how much you wanted him, Jenny."

"That was an awful thing to do, Daddy!"

"Yes it was, but then when his father saw him teasing Bubby and being mean to him, he decided to do something about it. That's when he decided to see if he could bring Bubby back to us. He could tell how devastated you were when you handed him over to me." Jenny's father swallowed hard. "I offered to give him his money back, but he wouldn't take it, and insisted that we keep it."

"Well, that was nice," Jake said.

"Yes, it was, Jake. And he also told us this had really opened his eyes, and that things around his house were going to be a lot different from now on!"

Jenny's mother added, "The hard part was keeping Bubby hidden from you until this morning! We decided to keep him inside for the night, so Grandma fixed up a little place for him in the guest room closet."

Grandma added, "And then we crossed our fingers he'd be quiet so we could surprise you!"

"Aww, it was the best surprise ever! I thought maybe I was just dreaming. I still can't believe it!"

Then Jake asked his father, "So then what happened to little Brownie?"

"Well, it seems Mr. Williams' mother fell in love with Brownie and wanted to keep her. He was glad, because now she would have a little companion to live with her."

"Aww, that makes me happy to know Brownie has a nice home now. I just knew that man looked like a good person," Jenny said. Jenny held Bubby close to her, gently stroking his soft golden coat. "I love you all so much. This is the best

Christmas I ever, ever had!" Then she stopped, looked up at her father, and asked, "Daddy? Are you going to let me keep Bubby this time?"

Mr. Johnson took a deep breath and then answered, "Yes, honey, I am. I should never have let him go in the first place, and I'm real sorry."

With a big sigh of relief, Jenny smiled and turned her gaze to the flickering flames in the fireplace and thought, *Maybe it was the Magic 8-Ball, or the Christmas snow, or maybe there really is a Santa Claus after all.* But deep down inside, Jenny was thankful that her prayers had been answered.

CHAPTER 11

THE NEXT MORNING was bitterly cold and very windy, with threatening snow clouds scattered across the dark-gray sky. But that wasn't enough to stop the determined Johnson men from braving the outdoors.

"Okay, Jake, are you ready to try out that new rifle?"

"I sure am, Dad! Gramps, you're coming too, right?"

"You know I am," Grandpa replied. "I wouldn't miss this for nothin'! Are we taking Shadow along with us?"

"Yes, Pop, I think we will. She'd get a real kick out of that. She used to go hunting with me and Martha's dad all the time. Come to think about it, I don't think she's been out in the fields since we lost him this spring."

"Well, not counting our Christmas tree excursion a couple weeks ago," Jake added. Bundled up in multiple layers of clothes, the three generations of Johnsons were geared up for a blizzard but could barely move their arms or legs.

"Now be sure to keep this scarf up around your face," Jake's mother told him as she wrapped him up tightly.

"Mom! I can't see anything! I look like a mummy, and I walk like a penguin!"

"Well, I just don't want any of you coming down with pneumonia, that's all. It is so cold outside today."

Mr. Johnson gave his wife a reassuring peck on the cheek. "Relax, dear. We'll be just fine."

They managed to navigate the front porch stairs, across the snow-covered driveway, and over to the barn. Shadow was standing by the barn door looking up at them, wagging her tail in anticipation. She could sense what was about to happen, and welcomed the awkward-looking trio with a few loud barks. Shadow was so excited she shivered from head to tail, and the hair on the scruff of her neck stood straight up.

Behind the barn at the edge of the cornfield, Jake's father sat three empty tin cans on top of some old cedar fence posts. Then he came back and stood next to Jake.

"Now, Jake, remember the safety rules your grandpa and I talked to you about yesterday?"

"Yeah, Dad, I remember."

"Well this .22 rifle is a little different than that BB gun you're used to, so I want you to pay real close attention to what I tell you. You already know about keeping the safety on until you're ready to aim and fire. And never point your gun at anyone, not even if it's unloaded."

"Dad! We went over that stuff yesterday, remember?" Jake was cold and becoming restless while his father continued talking.

"And remember, a firearm is a dangerous weapon, and you must always take proper safety measures when using one."

"Yes, Dad. I understand. I know I need to be careful and responsible."

"Well, now we need to give you some pointers on aiming. And then you can shoot at some sitting targets before we try stuff that moves."

"Okay, Dad."

"Now, hold the barrel with your left palm beneath it, elbow in, and raise the stock to your right shoulder. That's right... Now use the scope to get your target in sight. You can take the safety off now, but don't forget, you've already got a bullet in the chamber." Jake followed his father's instructions. "When you've carefully aimed and have your target in the center of the crosshairs, raise the gun slightly above the target... That's right, and now exhale. Okay, lower the barrel slowly without taking another breath, aim...and gently squeeze the trigger."

Blaaam! Jake hit his first target dead center, sending the empty soup can flying off the fence post to the frozen ground. Shadow let out an approving howl.

"Wow! Let me try that again!" Jake aimed carefully, repeating what his father had told him, and two more cans went flying.

"Atta boy, Jake!" Grandpa shouted. "I'm gonna have to start calling you Shooter." He laughed.

Jake's father praised him and continued, "Yes, it looks like you're ready to go hunting. Let's try to head out toward the pond and see if Shadow can flush something up for us." The optimistic hunters trudged at a snail's pace through the plowed cornfield, which had been lush, green, and full of sweet corn the summer before. There was nothing left now but rows of bent, severed stalks covered with ice and snow. In hopes of stumbling across a moving target, the only thing they stumbled across were their own frozen feet. Each step required more effort than the one before, as the icy cold winds swirled around them.

"D-d-d-dad, m-m-m-maybe w-w-w-we should w-w-w-wait till it g-g-g-gets a little w-w-w-warmer!"

"M-m-m-m-maybe you're r-r-r-right, J-J-J-Jake!"

As quickly as humanly possible, they struggled to make their way back to the warmth of the farmhouse, shuddering and shivering as they went. Each word, each groan, each exhaled breath became trapped in midair, suspended in front of them like a puff of steam before evaporating into thin air. Even Shadow seemed relieved to be getting out of the cold windy field as she scurried back to the protection of the big red barn. Mrs. Johnson, Grandma, and Jenny could hear the loud stomping in the mudroom.

"Well, that didn't last long," Jenny said and then giggled. The kitchen door creaked open slowly as the so-glad-to-be-back-inside-the-house bodies stepped inside to the warmth and comforts of home.

"G-g-g-good gravy, Marie! It must be forty below zero out there," Grandpa exclaimed while they all hurried to unbundle themselves.

"Well, I hate to say I told you so, but—" Mrs. Johnson teased.

"Oh, don't rub it in, dear. How about a little something to warm me up here?" Mr. Johnson put his cold hands on his wife's neck, sending a chill down her spine.

"Ooh quit that! Your fingers are like icicles! What you need is a nice hot cup of coffee!"

Jake joined his sister by the fireplace. She'd spread out a newspaper on the floor and was trying her hand at a paint-by-number picture. Bubby was curled up in a ball next to her, sound asleep. "Well, I don't know about anyone else, but I think I'll just stay in here with you where it's warm!"

Jake reached under the Christmas tree, pulled out one of his new dragon books, and plopped down next to Jenny. "I'll be so glad when spring gets here so I can go hunting for real. I know Dad and Gramps were just trying to help today, but I already know how to hunt."

"But you haven't had much practice shooting, have you, Jake?" asked Jenny.

"Whaddya mean? I've been shooting my BB gun since I was nine. And today I hit every single can with my new .22 rifle."

"I dunno, Jake. You'd just better be careful, that's all." Jenny shook her head and frowned at her brother.

"Blah blah blah. You sound more like a parent than a little sister!" Jake snapped.

They stuck their tongues out at each other in fun and continued with their painting and reading.

CHAPTER 12

IT WAS EXCITING news when Grandpa and Grandma Johnson announced they were going to stay another week. They had decided to wait to go home until after New Year's. And as Jake and Jenny had hoped, the following week was filled with a lot of fun, laughter, and plenty of Grandpa's imaginative stories.

"Hey, Gramps?" Jake asked on New Year's Eve. "How about telling us again about the time you shot that grizzly bear up in the mountains. That's my favorite story!" Jake got down on the floor next to his grandpa's chair. Lying on his stomach, he propped his chin on his fists and gave Grandpa his full attention as everyone else settled in for one of Grandpa's long-winded tales.

"Well, this ought to be good." Grandma snickered as she crossed her arms and leaned back in her rocking chair. "I swear, this story gets better every time you tell it!"

Grandpa laughed and said, "Well, let's see now." He looked over at Grandma and gave her a little wink. Then he settled back in the brown leather recliner and continued.

"Well now, back when I was a young fella, my Uncle Henry had an old log cabin on some land up in the Pocono Mountains. I always looked forward to going there to visit him. Come to think about it, I wasn't much bigger than you two kids when I used to go stay with him for a week or so during the summer."

Jake shifted positions and grinned. *Okay, here's the part when Gramps starts talking real funny.*

Grandpa continued with his storytelling. "Then some years later, poor old Uncle Henry kicked the bucket. And believe it or not, he left me that cabin in his last will and testament, bless his soul. So I figured I'd go and see for myself if the old place was still standin'. Yessir, it sure was good to get up in those mountains again. I made sure I had everything I'd need up there. Had a couple of pots and pans, some matches, a kerosene lantern, a warm blanket, a fishin' pole, and my double-barrel shotgun. Oh, and a pair or two of clean underwear."

Jenny giggled and covered her head with one of the pillows from the couch as her grandpa continued. "Every mornin', I'd go down to the creek and catch a fish and fry it up for my breakfast. Some days I'd get lucky and find some walnuts or wild berries. Come suppertime I'd shoot me a squirrel or a possum, or some critter like that. Then I'd skin it, clean it, and cook it up over my campfire. My favorite was a nice rabbit stew with morel mushrooms and soda biscuits on the side!"

Jake squirmed restlessly. *Come on, Gramps! Hurry up and get to the part about the bear!*

"Now one mornin', I was standin' next to a big old pine tree alongside the creek tryin' to catch a fish. And I was just about to catch the biggest, purtiest trout I ever did see when all of a sudden, I heard some fierce growling comin' from behind me! So I turned around to see what was makin' all that racket. And that's when I saw it!"

"Saw what, Grandpa?" Jenny asked.

"Well, let me tell ya. It was without a doubt the biggest, the ugliest, and the meanest grizzly bear I'd ever set my eyes on. Course there wasn't a whole lot I could do with nothin' but a fishin' pole in my hand. So I snuck around to the other side of that tree and made a run for the cabin to get my shot-gun. And boy oh boy, let me tell ya, that bear started chasin' me all the way to the front porch. He got so close I could feel his hot breath goin' down the back of my neck."

Yay, here comes my favorite part! Jake thought.

"Then, just when he got right on top of me"—Grandpa paused—"I grabbed my shotgun off the porch, swung around, pointed the gun up in the air so's to scare him off, and BOOOOM! Somehow, I shot that scoundrel right between his ears! That old grizzly didn't know what was happenin' and neither did I. He looked at me, and I looked back at him standin' there with a big smokin' bald patch on the top of his head."

"Oh, Grandpa! Ewww!" Jenny let out a little squeal and covered up again with the couch pillow. Jake's eyes lit up, and Grandpa laughed as he continued.

"Before I knew it, that bear turned around and high-tailed it off into the woods, howlin' all the way. 'Yeah, and don't come back!' I yelled at him. I reckon there's a bald-headed old bear still running around in the woods to this day."

"Oh, Grandpa! That poor bear!" Jenny cried.

"Ah, don't you worry, honey. It all happened so fast he never felt a thing!"

"If you say so, Grandpa!"

"Anyway, I was feelin' real proud of myself right about then. That's when I looked down on the ground, and there, layin' at my feet, sat this hunk of dark-brown fur. And it was still smokin'. Turns out it had come clean off that bear's head in one big piece."

Grandpa's story was interrupted by Grandma. She was rocking back and forth in her rocking chair, making fake snoring sounds with her eyes closed.

"Okay, okay, I'm almost to the end!" Grandpa chuckled. "Now where was I? Oh yes, I remember. So me and your grandma were just courtin' at the time, and I got this idea that maybe I could impress her if I made her somethin' out of that fur. That's when I took a piece of twelve-pound test line and then made a needle out of a big fish bone. I wanted to make her a nice fur coat. Course, as it turned out, I only had enough fur to make a little hat, but that would just have to do. Soon as I got back home about a week later, I went right over to your grandma's house and handed her that hat."

"And did Grandma like her little hat, Grandpa?" Jenny asked.

"Well, let me tell ya. At first she was speechless and didn't know what to say. Then she admitted she'd never seen one like it! That's when I got down on my good knee and asked her to marry me. And she was so thrilled, she agreed to marry me right then and there—but on one condition."

"What condition, Grandpa?" Jake asked.

"She made me promise I'd never make her another hat like that. So I promised I wouldn't, and she said 'Then yes, I will,' and we did, and that is exactly how it happened."

"Grandma! Now is that really true?"

Grandma winked at Jenny and then chuckled and said, "Well, I suppose it is...give or take a little white lie or two."

As Jenny laughed at her grandparents, she noticed the time. "Hurry, everybody, it's almost midnight!" Jenny's father turned on the television to a special New Year's Eve show. Grandma handed out the noisemakers and paper party hats to everyone.

"Okay, come on now! It's time! Ten, nine, eight, seven..." They all counted down the seconds together and then shouted out, "Happy New Year! Happy New Year, everybody!" Jake paid no attention to the rest of the family as they sang "Auld Lang Syne." He was caught up in an imaginary world of his own, in another time. In his mind, he was up at that old cabin in the mountains with his new rifle, coming face-to-face with that big bald grizzly bear.

CHAPTER 13

AS THE WINTER days were winding down and growing longer, Bubby was growing bigger and stronger. Although he was still smaller than the average Labrador puppy at five months, he was very smart and a quick learner. With spring just around the corner, Jake and his father would soon be plowing up the fields. In the meantime, Mr. Johnson prepared income taxes for some small private companies back in Cedar Falls. The family's future was looking brighter, and they were eager to plant a new crop of corn.

Bubby was still learning how to fetch a stick and bring it to Jenny. "You are such a good boy," Jenny praised him. "It won't be long till you'll be as good at this as your mommy!" Shadow liked joining Jenny and Bubby on their outings around the farm.

One Saturday afternoon, while playing in the yard, Jenny called, "Come here, Bubby! Let's see if you can run and get this big stick before your mommy can. Ready, set, go!" Bubby took off running as fast as his little legs would carry him. Shadow gracefully ambled over to where Jenny had thrown the stick and picked it up in her mouth. Then she pranced up to Jenny and dropped it on the ground in front of her feet. Realizing his mother had already gotten the stick, Bubby quickly turned around and raced back toward them. He was about five feet in front of Jenny and Shadow when he tripped and fell forward, landing on his chin.

"Aww, you poor little thing!" Jenny scooped him up off the ground and brushed away the dirt with her fingers. "I guess you're gonna have to keep practicing some more before you'll be able to beat your mommy to those sticks. But we'll teach you how, won't we, girl?" Shadow looked up at Jenny and wagged her tail in agreement. "It's a lot warmer than usual today! I think this is what they call a false spring. Let's take a nice long walk and enjoy the sunshine and the fresh air," Jenny said to her two companions.

It was such a beautiful day that Jenny really didn't want to go back to the farmhouse yet. Wandering leisurely past the barn, across the cornfield, and past a stand of poplar trees, they came to a small creek. They followed it to where it flowed into the large pond where they had gone skating during the winter.

The brisk March winds whipped across the meadow and through Jenny's soft brown hair as she played with Bubby and Shadow. She sat down near the edge of the water and looked up at the clouds in the beautiful blue sky. As she enjoyed the warmth of the sun shining down on her freckled cheeks, she was suspended in time without a care in the world, in the fragile, carefree days of her youth.

"Yes, Dad. I'll be careful!" said Jake, clutching his .22 rifle with his right hand and stuffing as many bullets as he could into the pocket of his denim jacket. Jake was excited to be taking his rifle out by himself. First he went over by the barn to practice, but he soon got bored shooting tin cans off of fence posts.

The sun's rays felt as warm and welcoming to Jake as they did to Jenny. *Ah, now this is more like it! I think I'll go over to the woods and see if I can scare up some birds, or maybe even a squirrel or a rabbit.* His excitement was building, his heart beginning to beat a little faster as he tramped across the field. He could see the beckoning woods in the distance. As he walked, he daydreamed, his young mind full of the wishful creations of his imagination. He was young and energetic and out to prove he was capable of doing a lot more than people gave him credit for.

Jake approached the edge of the woods and proceeded to shimmy up a tall, stately sycamore tree, which was no easy task in itself. His rifle was cumbersome as he clutched it under his left arm, leaving only his right arm free for pulling and climbing. Finally, he reached the top branches of the tree, which gave him a panoramic view of the fields and pastures below.

"Oh wow! I can see everything from up here. Over there's our house and my bedroom window, the barn, the workshop, the equipment shed...and I can even see the big pond from way up here!"

In the distance, and out of the corner of his eye, Jake noticed something move slightly in the tall weeds near the edge of the pond.

"Oh boy! There's something pretty big over there! It could be a deer, maybe!"

He raised his rifle up to his shoulder, released the safety, and raised the barrel of the gun slightly, exhaling just as his father had taught him. With a steady hand and an accurate eye, he aimed and gently squeezed the trigger.

Whatever it was that had been rustling in the weeds before did not move now. It wasn't until the pinging sound of the bullet cleared from his ears that Jake could hear a distressed, helpless shriek coming from the vicinity of the pond. Jake was suddenly overcome with a sickening emptiness in his stomach. He instantly dropped his rifle to the ground and scrambled down the tree in a panic. He ran as fast as he could, heading toward the pond. *Oh no...what have I done?* Jake kept repeating that thought over and over in his head. As he reached the edge of the water, his heart was pounding hard in his chest, and then it quickly sank as he found his sister, Jenny, slumped over in the tall grass.

CHAPTER 14

❧

JENNY SOBBED AS she slowly rocked back and forth, crying out helplessly for someone to help her. Jake was surprised to see Shadow's head resting in Jenny's lap. Shadow's body appeared limp and lifeless. Jenny used her hand to try to wipe away the fresh blood coming from just above the Labrador's left ear.

"Jenny! Are you all right? Are you bleeding?"

"Jaaaaake, please help meeeeeee! I'm okay, but something awful has happened to Shadow. She's bleeding, Jake! Please...please help me get her home!" Jenny sobbed.

"Shh, don't cry, Jenny. It's going to be okay. Come on. I'll carry Shadow for you. I'm sure everything will be okay." Jake pulled out the red bandana he had stuffed into his left pants pocket. Then he carefully tied it around Shadow's head to help control the bleeding. He bit his bottom lip, not having the courage to tell his sister the truth about what was going on. *I can't believe this happened! I don't dare say a word to Jenny. She'll never, ever forgive me. I don't think I'll ever forgive myself either!*

A lump formed in his throat as he carefully picked up Shadow. She was like a dead weight in his arms, and it was all he could do to lift her up. Little Bubby could sense something was wrong. Jenny scooped him up into her arms, and the four of them started plodding their way back to the farmhouse. Shadow's body felt lifeless and heavy in Jake's arms. He carefully shifted her weight from one arm to the other as they walked. Side by side they continued. It was the longest walk either of the Johnson children had ever taken together, each passing moment filled with confusion and regrets.

Jenny ran ahead to get their parents. Jake struggled as he carried Shadow into the barn and over to the corner stall that had always been a place where Shadow felt safe and secure. He knelt down and lowered her gently onto a soft mound of straw, trying to make her as comfortable as possible. He held his cheek up close to Shadow's mouth and could feel faint puffs of air coming from her nose and mouth.

"She's still breathing! Thank God she's still alive."

Moments later, Mr. and Mrs. Johnson rushed into the barn with Jenny right on their heels.

"We've phoned Doc Wilson and he's on his way. We're lucky he was just up the road at Jim Howard's ranch," said Mr. Johnson.

"So, Jake, do you know what happened?" his father asked, as he knelt down next to Shadow. A silence fell over the barn as he removed the blood-soaked bandana. He looked up with a frown and stared right into his son's eyes.

"I'm not sure what happened, Dad. All I know is I heard Jenny scream and I ran out to the pond to see what was wrong." Jake's father could always tell when one of his children was not being completely truthful with him.

"You need to go outside and watch for Doc Wilson."

"Yes, Dad," Jake agreed and stood up to leave.

"Jacob William..."

"Sir?"

"Go on up to your room after Doc gets here. I'll come see you after he's finished with Shadow."

"Yes, sir," Jake replied, his head held low, his spirit lifted from him. *I'm really in trouble now! I was going to tell the truth about what happened...I really was. I just couldn't say anything in front of Jenny.*

Doc Wilson was an elderly gentleman, somewhere in his early seventies. As he pulled his car into the Johnsons' driveway, Jake waved to him and pointed over to the barn. Then he went inside and up to his room as he was told. The old doctor struggled slightly as he opened his car door and stepped out onto the gravel in the driveway. He walked slowly toward the barn, his narrow shoulders stooped over from age. The old leather doctor's bag he carried by his side was every bit as weathered as his aged hands. Mr. Johnson came out of the barn to greet his old family friend and then took him in to where Shadow was resting.

"We're glad you could make it here so soon. Can you take a look at her, Doc?" Despite the stiffness in his knees, Doc Wilson knelt down next to Shadow. He placed his doctor's bag beside him and opened it up. Jenny could see a lot of complicated-looking medical instruments inside. The doctor reached in and pulled out his stethoscope. He put the two long ends into his ears and held the shiny round bottom piece over Shadow's heart. For what seemed like forever to Jenny, Doc Wilson examined Shadow. He listened to her heart and lungs. Then he lifted up her eyelids to look at her pupils, and probed carefully around the bleeding area near her ear. Pulling his stethoscope down from his ears, Doc Wilson shook his head as he slowly stood up.

"So...how does she look, Doc?" Jenny's father asked.

Doc Wilson cleared his throat and hesitated before responding. "I'm afraid it doesn't look very promising, Bill. She has fairly good vital signs, but it's lodged in there pretty good. She won't survive if it stays in there much longer." Jenny overheard the doctor and walked over next to him to listen in on the conversation. "I'm not an expert at modern techniques, you know. These shaky old hands of mine would probably do more damage than good if I were to try and go in there and take it out."

"Take what out?" Jenny interrupted. "What are you talking about?" Her father walked over next to her and put his hand on her shoulder.

Doc Wilson continued, "You might want to consider your options. If you want me to, I could go ahead and put her down for you while I'm here."

"Noooooo!" Jenny wailed. "What do you mean? Daddy! Don't let her be killed! And you can't let her die. Daddy, you've got to do something... Daddy, please!"

"Now listen, Jenny, I'm sure Doctor Wilson is doing everything he can for Shadow." He patted her shoulder, trying to console her.

"Well, just a minute, Bill. I may have spoken a bit soon. You know, I have seen a few cases like this where an animal survived this type of gunshot wound."

"Daddy! What?"

"Shh, not now Jenny."

Doc Wilson paused and then said, "We shouldn't move her too far right now. I'll give her something strong for pain before I go, and I'll leave some for you to give her later on tonight."

"We appreciate that, Doc," said Mr. Johnson.

"I'll come back in the morning and bring that young Tim Richards with me. He's a new vet over at Cedar Falls, and he might be able to help her where I can't."

"Oh, that sounds good, Doc. Let's do that."

"Okay then. I'm giving her two of these white pills now for pain, and you need to give her two more in about six hours from now. Try to get her to eat something, and do your best to get her to drink some water if you can. It's very important that you do that."

"We will, Doc," Jenny's father replied.

"Thank you, Doctor Wilson," Jenny said.

As he drove out of the driveway, the doctor waved to the Johnsons and called out, "I'll see you folks in the morning."

Jenny looked up at her father and started rolling off a list of questions.

"Daddy, what was he talking about? He said something about a gunshot! Did he really mean Shadow was shot with a gun? How could that have happened? Who could do a thing like that?"

"Hey, slow down! One question at a time, please!" Her father tried to avoid answering her questions for the moment and replied, "I'm sure whatever happened out there was an accident, honey. The important thing now is that we let Shadow rest for a while. We'll come out after supper to see if we can get her to eat something. You just try not to worry." But her father knew things were not that simple, and there was plenty to worry about. Bubby curled up next to his mother as Jenny reached over and grabbed her father's hand. They left the barn without saying a word.

CHAPTER 15

IT WAS ALMOST time for supper when Mr. Johnson knocked on Jake's bedroom door, cracking it open slightly. "Jake, I'm ready to talk to you now."

"Come on in, Dad." His father could tell Jake was very upset. His eyes were red from crying, his cheeks still damp from his tears. "How is Shadow? What did Doc Wilson say?" Jake asked.

Mr. Johnson sat on the bed next to Jake and said, "Well, it's really too soon to tell, but it's very serious. We're hoping she'll make it through the night. Doc Wilson is coming back in the morning, and then we'll just have to take it from there." More tears began to roll down Jake's cheeks as his father continued. "Jake, I want you to tell me the truth this time about what happened out there this afternoon."

"I didn't want to lie." Jake looked up at his father sadly and continued. "I wanted to tell you right away, but I just couldn't talk about it in front of Jenny."

"You mean about you shooting Shadow?"

"Yes. It was me. You know I did it. It was a stupid, careless mistake." Jake got up and grabbed a clean tissue out of the box on his dresser. He blew his nose and then continued. "Dad, I never meant for anything like that to happen! You believe me, don't you? It was all an accident!"

"Yes, Jake, I'm sure it was. Accidents happen because someone has been careless. It's plain and simple. Please understand, I'm not angry at you, Jake. It's just that I am so...so disappointed in you." Jake winced as he listened to his father's stinging words. "What if that bullet had hit your sister instead of Shadow? Do you realize how close you came to shooting your own sister today? I just don't understand... I thought you were ready to go out there on your own. And I thought I'd done everything I could to make sure you could handle that rifle safely...that you knew how and how not to handle a firearm."

"You did, Dad. You taught me all of that stuff. I guess I was just trying to prove something to everybody—prove I was growing up now, and wasn't just a dumb kid." Jake sniffled and continued. "I've done a real lousy job of that, haven't I?"

"Jake, it takes a lot of courage to admit to a mistake. You're a smart boy, and you're growing into a responsible young man. Otherwise, I never would have trusted you with a rifle in the first place."

"Yeah, well, I never want to shoot or even see another gun again as long as I live! I know it was my Christmas present, but do whatever you want to with that rifle."

"Well, let's not go that far, Jake, because hopefully you'll change your mind someday. But you do understand I'll have to give you some sort of punishment for not telling the truth, right?" Jake nodded his head as he sat back down on the bed, stared down at the floor, and listened as his father continued. "Tomorrow, I want you to go out there and get your rifle and bring it to me. I'll put it up until I feel you've earned the privilege to have it back again. And I'll be finding plenty of extra work around the farm to keep you busy."

"That's fine with me, Dad. I don't mind. I just want Shadow to be okay. And I want you to know how sorry I am for what I've done." Jake paused. "And I hope you can forgive me."

"Of course I can forgive you, Jake. I already have." His father reached over and put an arm around him. "And I'm sure your sister will too, once she knows what really happened. You do know I expect you to own up to this and tell her the truth when you're ready."

"Yes, I'll tell her, I promise."

"One day you'll realize growing up wasn't as easy as you thought it would be."

"I can see that already, Dad!" said Jake.

"You're also going to find that some lessons can only be learned by experiencing them yourself, and learning from your own mistakes. I personally think you've done a lot of growing up today, Jake. What do you think?"

"Yeah, Dad, you're right. You always are."

Mr. Johnson clapped his hands together as he started to stand up from the bed. "Let's go get some supper! I smell pot roast!"

"Yes, sir! And afterwards I'll help Jenny with Shadow. I'll do anything I can to help Shadow get better. You can count on it."

CHAPTER 16

❧

"COME ON, GIRL, look what I have for you. You've gotta eat something to help you get well," Jenny said. She pleaded with Shadow to eat some leftover beef roast from supper. Jenny knew it was important for Shadow to get nourishment to keep her strength up. Shadow raised her head slightly, sniffed the food in Jenny's hand, and then gave out a small whine as she laid her head back down. Jake soon walked into the barn and over to where Shadow was laying.

"Did she eat anything yet, Jenny?"

"No, nothing. She can barely raise her head up. I don't know what we'll do if we can't get her to eat. See if she'll eat for you, Jake."

"I'll try, but I doubt if she'll eat for me if she wouldn't for you." Jake carefully put his hand under Shadow's head and whispered, "Okay, girl, you just lay there and I'll feed you." He slowly fed her some of the roast by hand. Shadow swallowed a few bites, as Jake continued feeding her. "Such a good girl! Yes, go on... Doesn't that taste good?" She managed to give her tail a meager thump.

"That's great, Jake. Here, let's see if she'll drink something." Jenny slid the water dish over next to Shadow. It took a lot of effort for Shadow to lap at the cool water with her tongue, but she managed to drink some of it. Exhausted, she laid her head down onto the soft straw, closed her eyes, and soon went back to sleep.

Jenny, Jake, and Bubby stayed with Shadow until it was time for her next dose of pain medicine. Jenny had watched how Doc Wilson gave the pills to Shadow that afternoon. With her father looking on, Jenny raised Shadow's chin, gently opened her mouth, and stuck the pills as far back into her throat as she could. She closed Shadow's mouth and massaged her throat until she swallowed and the pills went down. Then Shadow drank a few more laps of water.

"Good job, Jenny. That should keep her comfortable until morning," her father said.

"I sure hope so, Daddy. I feel really bad for her." Jenny stopped and then asked, "Would it be okay if Jake and I slept out here in the barn tonight? I don't want her to wake up hurting and scared and all alone."

"No, I'm afraid not. It'll be way too cold for that! Plus, I know your mother would never go for it. How about we compromise and bring Shadow inside for the night."

This news sent the kids scurrying to gather up some blankets, sleeping bags, and pillows. Mr. Johnson remembered what Doc Wilson had said about moving Shadow. He very carefully carried her from the barn and into the mudroom next to the kitchen. Jake and Jenny quickly made up their own pallets on the floor next to the comfortable spot they'd fixed up for Shadow. Making sure they were all settled in for the night, Mr. Johnson turned on a night light for them and switched off the overhead light in the mudroom.

"Now if something happens during the night, you kids come on upstairs and get your mother or me. We'll be right there if you need us."

"We will, Daddy. Thank you! Good night!" the kids called out in unison. They said their prayers and were soon sound asleep. Poor little Bubby knew something was terribly wrong. He stayed by his mother's side, frightened and curled up for dear life between her and Jenny. He finally closed his eyes and fell asleep too.

CHAPTER 17

Doc Wilson and the new vet from Cedar Falls arrived very early the next morning and started walking toward the barn. Mr. Johnson stuck his head out the screen door and motioned to the doctors. "Over here! We brought her inside with us last night," he said.

Tim Richards, a tall blonde-haired man in his early thirties, accompanied Doc Wilson into the mudroom. After introducing himself, he bent down next to Shadow and gave Bubby a little pat on the head. Jenny and Jake were awakened by the commotion. They rubbed their eyes and yawned sleepily as they sat up and began to watch with interest.

The young doctor began to softly speak to Shadow. "Hey there, girl," he whispered, as he took several of his instruments from his bag. "Let me just take a look." He began examining the area where the bullet was lodged. After a few minutes of probing and prodding he said, "Well, it will be tricky, but I'm going to give it a try. That bullet is lodged in there pretty good. I'll do my best to take it out without causing any more damage."

The Johnsons remained completely quiet as they listened to Dr. Richards. Even Jenny kept quiet and asked no questions. "Normally I'd do a difficult procedure like this at the animal hospital, but I really don't recommend moving her that far in the condition she's in."

"Is there anything we can do to help, Doc?" Mr. Johnson asked.

"Actually, it would probably be best if you folks went on about your business while I do this. And I'll be sure to call you when I've finished."

"Okay, you heard the doctor! Jake, go get yourself dressed. I could use your help with that old planter out in the barn. Jenny, why don't you go help your mother cook something." The children obeyed their father, reluctantly giving up their vigil over Shadow. Bubby stayed as close as he could to his mother. Old Doc Wilson held him on his lap while also holding a spotlight above Shadow. Dr. Richards sterilized the area around the gunshot wound to prepare for the operation. Once Shadow was fully sedated, he began to carefully remove the bullet.

"It's in a very...precarious...position here, but I think... Ahh, there it comes."

As he continued talking to Doc Wilson, he delicately eased out the bullet that had been lodged behind Shadow's left ear. "Got it! It's out!" Both doctors breathed a big sigh of relief as Dr. Richards released the bullet from his forceps, sending it clinking into the stainless steel pan on the floor next to him.

"Well, I don't have to tell you, I'm glad that's over. Very risky, and a really close call!" Doc Wilson agreed as he took Shadow's vital signs and then bandaged her head with some sterile white gauze to keep the wound clean and dry. Shadow had lost a little more blood during the surgery, so Dr. Richards wanted to be very careful to keep her as calm as possible. He poked his head through the doorway of the mudroom and into the kitchen.

"Okay, folks, we're finished now. Do you mind if we step into the kitchen here?"

"Come on in! That'll be just fine!" Mrs. Johnson replied. "Jenny, please go get your father and Jake and have them come here, too."

Soon, everyone was gathered around the kitchen table, anxious to hear what the doctors had to say. Mrs. Johnson served up a fresh cup of coffee to the adults as everyone took a seat. Dr. Richards glanced over at Doc Wilson, who gave him a nod. He then began to explain the situation to the Johnson family.

"So, let me start off by saying that I'm sure you all know how serious this injury was." He cleared his throat and continued, "But I think I have some good news for you! As far as I can tell, the operation itself was successful. She's still under heavy sedation, but her vitals are good and she seems to be sleeping comfortably." The Johnsons let out a collective sigh of relief as Dr. Richards continued. "I'm hoping no permanent damage was done, but it's really too soon to know for sure. I'll come out sometime next month and check on her. But in the meantime, if she gets a fever or won't eat, or if you notice anything that doesn't seem right, you need to call me right away."

Mr. Johnson reached out to shake the doctor's hand. "We can't thank you enough. Thanks to the both of you!"

"See, Bill! I told you he was sharp," Doc Wilson replied. "And you can see you'll be in good hands whenever I decide to retire!" With Bubby in her arms, Jenny followed her father and the doctors as they headed outside and walked down the backstairs.

"Take good care of your momma, little one," Dr. Richards said as he patted Bubby on his head one more time. Both doctors waved goodbye to the family as they pulled out of the driveway, heading back to Cedar Falls.

CHAPTER 18

OVER THE NEXT few days, Shadow's condition slowly began to improve. At first she moved around sluggishly but then gradually began regaining her strength. Every day when Jake and Jenny got home from school, the first thing they did was check on Shadow. Her appetite started to return after a few days, and after about a week, she started wandering outside the barn with Bubby at her side.

Dr. Richards came back the following month as he had promised. After a thorough examination, he was surprised but pleased to be able to give Shadow a clean bill of health. The doctor's good news made the family's Easter holiday even more joyous. It was almost like Shadow had been given a new chance at life after surviving her horrible ordeal.

Life slowly began returning to normal on the Johnson farm. The new crop of sweet corn was planted, and Jake stayed busy working off his punishment, but he did so with no argument or complaints. Shadow continued to improve, and Bubby continued to grow and learn new things. Jenny and Jake finished up their school year that June and were happy to have some time off to relax and enjoy themselves.

Jake eventually brought himself to tell his sister the truth about Shadow's accident. It was on a hot afternoon that July as the two of them were fishing down at the pond. Shadow had found a shady spot over by the edge of the woods and had sprawled out to take a nap. Bubby splashed playfully at the water's edge, keeping himself occupied by chasing after dragonflies and brown water spiders. On the far side of the pond, Mr. Johnson was taking a break from working to use the fishing rod Jenny had gotten him for Christmas.

"You know, Jake, I've been wondering why you don't want to go hunting anymore, and now I think I know why," Jenny said, carefully threading another worm onto her fishing hook.

"You do?" Jake replied.

"Yes, I do," she continued, plopping her line back into the water and wiping her fingers off in the grass. "I think it's because you don't want to hurt or kill animals for real. It's different when we go fishing. We just throw the little ones back and they grow up and we catch them again."

"Yeah, so?"

"Well when you shoot animals, it's different...because then they're either hurt or dead, and—"

Jake interrupted his sister, having finally, at that very moment, mustered up the courage to tell her about the accident.

"You're right, Jenny. I don't ever want to hurt an animal again...like I did when Shadow got shot." Jenny had been keeping a close eye on her bobber, which had been darting around in the water for a few seconds.

She glanced quickly over her shoulder at Jake. "Say that again?"

"I'm trying to tell you I was the one who shot Shadow. It was me, with my .22 rifle! But it was an accident, Jenny." Jake swallowed hard as he continued. "You know I'd never want to hurt anybody on purpose. And I sure didn't mean to hurt Shadow."

As Jake tried to explain, Jenny stopped him.

"Jake, please don't say any more. I figured out what happened a long time ago. And I know it had to have been an accident. You love Shadow just as much as I do! And Shadow's fine now, so you don't need to feel guilty or bad anymore." She walked up behind Jake, bent over, and put both arms around his neck. "Thank you for telling me, Jake. I know that must have been a hard thing for you to do."

"I wanted to tell you sooner. I guess there was never the right time till now. I'm really sorry, Jenny."

It was against Jenny's nature to hold a grudge against anyone. Besides, that was all behind them now. With the sun beginning to set, their father let out one of his loud whistles and held up a big string of largemouth bass. He waved to Jake and Jenny from across the pond to let them know he was heading back to the house.

"I guess we'd better be going too," Jake said. "I've got to feed the cows before supper! Looks to me like we might be having a fish fry!"

"Yum! I sure hope so," said Jenny. "Shadow! Bubby! It's time to go home now," Jenny called. Bubby, who was still chasing spiders, trotted over to her, his paws wet and muddy and his tail wagging. As Jake gathered up his can of worms and tackle box, Jenny looked around for Shadow. "I guess she's off taking a nap somewhere," she told Jake. "I called for her, but I don't see her." Jenny hadn't noticed that Bubby had wandered over toward the edge of the woods.

"I'm sure she'll be here in a minute," Jake assured her. Jake and Jenny started walking toward home, and soon Bubby and Shadow came running up behind them playfully.

"There you are, girl! You must have been sound asleep or having a really good dream!" Jenny said as they hiked onward. Jake felt a giant weight had now been lifted from his shoulders, and was glad he had finally told Jenny the truth. He reached over and tugged on one of her ponytails.

"Last one home's a deviled egg!"

"You mean rotten egg!" Jenny replied.

"Same difference!"

Jenny giggled at her brother, and squealed as she began to race him through the field, with Shadow and Bubby happily joining in on the chase.

CHAPTER 19

— ❦ —

ALTHOUGH JENNY KEPT trying to convince herself Shadow was fine, deep down inside, she had a feeling something was not right. Some days when Jenny walked into the barn, Shadow wouldn't get up to greet her like she used to. It wasn't until Bubby ran up to Jenny that Shadow noticed she was there. And even though Shadow could still run and fetch like she used to, there was definitely something different about her. Jenny mentioned it to her parents one night during supper.

"Maybe we should call Dr. Richards to come check her out again this weekend, just to make sure," her father suggested. "He'll be able to tell us if something is wrong or not."

That Saturday morning, after Dr. Richards finished examining Shadow, Jenny's fears were confirmed. He walked over from the barn and sat down on the steps to the front porch where Jenny and her parents were waiting. Brushing his fingers through his hair, he looked down and then shook his head slowly.

"Well, I'm afraid it's not the kind of news you wanted to hear. I hate having to say this, but I guess that bullet caused some permanent damage after all." Mr. Johnson sat down on the porch step next to Dr. Richards.

"So what can you tell us, Doc?"

"Her vital signs are normal, and her vision is really good for a dog her age, but"—the doctor hesitated—"I could tell you more with a full exam in my office, but I do know there is a problem with her hearing. Actually, I'm almost certain Shadow is deaf." The young doctor's words hung over him like an unwelcome storm cloud.

"But you can fix her, can't you?" Jenny pleaded. "I know you can!"

"Do you think there'd be anything you could do for her, Doc?" Mr. Johnson asked.

"To be honest, there's not really anything that can be done, without major surgery. And even if we were able to operate, I'm not sure it would be worth the huge risk. The chances of success in restoring her hearing would be fairly slim. And at her age..."

"Doc, can you tell if she's in any kind of pain?" asked Mr. Johnson.

"Well, that's the good thing. She doesn't appear to be in any apparent pain, and her hearing loss isn't life-threatening. I'd say she's still got some good years left in her, and there's no reason she won't be able to live them fully."

About that time, Jake had finished his chores in the barn and came up to the house to join the others. Dr. Richards nodded to Jake and then picked up his doctor's bag as he began to leave.

"Do dogs understand sign language?" Jenny asked.

"Well, not without being taught, but I'm sure she could catch on pretty quickly to your hand signals. I know of some books you can read on the subject if you'd be interested."

Having just joined the conversation, Jake was confused. "What are you guys talking about? Why do we need to do sign language?" Jake asked.

"For Shadow. Shadow can't hear anymore, Jake. She's deaf now," Jenny replied.

Jake stared at Jenny in disbelief, and had heard all he wanted to hear. He turned in anger, and started running back across the driveway toward the barn. He was stricken once again with a terrible sense of guilt. "It's all my fault!" he shouted. "This can't be happening!"

Jenny raced after her brother. Upset by the doctor's news but understanding Jake's reaction, she ran to catch up with him. She finally started getting closer to him, and watched him run between two rows of corn and into the open pasture ahead.

"Jake, wait! Stop! Please let me talk to you!" Jenny called. Shadow and Bubby eagerly followed Jenny, thinking it was just another one of their playful adventures out in the fields. By now, Jake was out of breath and unable to run any further. He stopped and collapsed onto the ground. Shadow and Bubby dashed right past Jenny and caught up with Jake. They jumped up on top of him and playfully tugged at his clothes. Jenny had to giggle as she watched them trampling all over her brother.

"Hey, cut it out!" Jake grumbled, and then began to laugh as Shadow licked his nose.

"See, Jake? Shadow can still have fun and play! It's all right! Shadow has you, and me...and Bubby! Bubby will look out for his momma." Jenny walked over to Jake and crouched down next to him. "Bubby can be Shadow's ears, and he'll be there to let her know if someone's coming. He'll get her attention if there's danger." Jenny offered her hand to help Jake.

"Everything's going to be fine. It really will, I promise!" Jake lay there silently for a moment and then slowly extended his hand to his sister. After Jenny helped him up, he brushed the grass and dirt off of himself and then hugged his little sister.

"Maybe you're right, Jenny. At least I hope you are."

"I know I'm right! Now come on, Jake. Let's go!" As they headed toward home, Jenny turned to her brother and exclaimed, "Hey, Jake! I almost forgot! Grandma and Grandpa Johnson are gonna be here next week! Remember?"

"Uh, no! Nobody told me anything about them coming. Who told you that?"

"Oops! I forgot I wasn't supposed to know about it. I heard Daddy talking to Grandpa about it on the phone a few weeks ago. Umm, it was supposed to be a surprise."

"You are way too nosy, Jenny! Someday you're going to get in so much trouble! But I'm glad you told me anyway. I can't wait to see them again!"

"I know! It seems like so long since they were here," Jenny agreed. "But you've got to promise to act surprised when they show up, okay?"

"Don't worry, I'll act surprised. I bet Gramps will really be surprised to see how much taller I've gotten since last Christmas."

"Yeah, Jake, I bet so, too! Maybe this time you and Daddy and Grandpa can go out to the woods and go hunting for real."

Jake hesitated. "I don't think I could do that. I don't know if I'll ever be able to do that."

"Come on," Jenny objected. "Why not? Besides, if you don't feel like shooting your gun, who says you have to? You could still just go along with them and do some of that bonding stuff or something."

Shadow walked up to Jake and nudged his hand and then trotted over to where Bubby was chasing down the bullfrog he saw jump into some tall weeds by the pond. "See! Even Shadow thinks you should go hunting," Jenny said.

"Well...maybe. Maybe I'll think about it." Through the shoulder-high rows of sweet corn, Jake and Jenny began their walk together through the fields, back to their home. Little Bubby nudged Shadow's left hind leg with his cold black nose to get her attention. They were quickly side by side with the children and joined them as they walked.

"Aw, did you see that, Jake?"

"Yeah, I saw." Jake smiled as he answered.

From that moment on, Jake and Jenny both knew that even though Shadow may have lost her hearing, she still had the two of them, and her little Bubby. And while Bubby may not have been very big in size, he had an enormous heart that was filled with a very special kind of love for his mother. And that little puppy's love was exactly what Shadow needed.

Once again, the foursome finished that long journey home together. This time it was in triumph. Almost a year had passed since Bubby had come into their lives. Not only had Jake gotten taller and wiser, but he had grown up. And his little sister had done a lot of growing up herself. It had been a year filled with minor tragedies and major victories—a year full of memories Jake and Jenny would hold on to for the rest of their lives.

ABOUT THE AUTHOR

DEBBIE WALTERS CULL developed her love of writing at an early age, excelling in various creative writing classes during her school years. She enjoys creating scripts for plays, local TV/radio commercials and has had several articles and poems published in current magazines and circulars. She is now fondly known for writing poignant stories and amusing anecdotes shared on various multimedia sources. Her writings have been described as "giving the reader a front-row seat. Her work is engaging and always leaves us wanting more.

Now that Debbie is retired from thirty years in the customer service field in the corporate world, she finally has the time she has yearned for to continue her writing career. Recently widowed after a very interesting life with her loving husband of thirty-six years, she uses writing to help heal and occupy her mind. She resides in the North Georgia Mountains in their beautiful little cabin with her Shih Tzu named Meeshu. Having raised four boys who are now all married with their own families, Debbie is relishing the opportunity to devote her undivided attention to her writing.

CPSIA information can be obtained
at www.ICGtesting.com
Printed in the USA
BVHW071242020821
613410BV00006B/140

9 781662 441479